W9-ARW-655

The Berenstain Bears®
Spring Storybook Collection

Stan & Jan Berenstain with Mike Berenstain

HARPER

An Imprint of HarperCollinsPublishers

The Berenstain Bears Spring Storybook Collection
Copyright © 2017 by Berenstain Publishing, Inc.
All rights reserved.

The Berenstain Bears' Lemonade Stand
Copyright © 2014 by Berenstain Publishing, Inc.

The Berenstain Bears' Easter Parade
Copyright © 2014 by Berenstain Publishing, Inc.

The Berenstain Bears Clean House
Copyright © 2005 by Berenstain Bears, Inc.

The Berenstain Bears Go Green
Copyright © 2013 by Berenstain Publishing, Inc.

The Berenstain Bears: Gone Fishin'!
Copyright © 2014 by Berenstain Publishing, Inc.

The Berenstain Bears: We Love Our Mom!
Copyright © 2012 by Berenstain Bears, Inc.

The Berenstain Bears: We Love Our Dad!
Copyright © 2013 by Berenstain Publishing, Inc.

Manufactured in China.
No part of this book may be used or reproduced in any manner whatsoever without written permission
except in the case of brief quotations embodied in critical articles and reviews. For information address
HarperCollins Children's Books, a division of HarperCollins Publishers, 195 Broadway, New York, NY 10007.

ISBN 978-0-06-243458-6

17 18 19 20 SCP 10 9 8 7 6 5 4 3 2   ❖   First Edition

CONTENTS

It is a hot day.

Brother, Sister, and Honey Bear
play outside.

Mama brings them lemonade.

Ahh! It is good.

Mailbear Bob comes by.

He is very hot.

"May I have some

lemonade?" he asks.

"I will give you a quarter."

Mailbear Bob drinks the lemonade.

Ahh! It is good.

"Here is your quarter," he says.

"Let's sell more lemonade,"
says Brother.

The cubs set up a lemonade stand.

They make a sign:

"Lemonade—25 cents."

Some bears are mowing

the lawn next door.

They are very hot.

They see the lemonade stand.

"We would like some lemonade,"
say the lawn bears.

They drink it down.

Ahh! It is good.

Their neighbor comes outside.

"I am having a party," she says.

"My guests will all want

lemonade."

Her guests arrive.

They all drink lemonade.

Ahh! It is good.

LEMONADE 25¢

Brother, Sist
+ Honey Bear

Some other neighbors come outside.

They want lemonade, too.

But the cubs are running out of

lemonade.

"Don't worry!" say the neighbors.

"We will help."

24

They bring out more drinks.

They bring out food to eat.

Some cubs come by.

"A block party!" they say.

They start to play music.

They start to dance.

It is a big party!

Farmer Ben sees the party.

He has a load of things from his farm.

He starts to sell fruit and other good things.

29

It is getting dark.

How will the party end?

Grizzly Gus has fireworks.

He sets them off.

They are very pretty!

The party is over.

Everyone goes home.

The cubs take down their
lemonade stand.
They go inside.
They are very tired.
They are very hot.

Mama brings them lemonade.

Ahh! It is good.

"That will be twenty-five cents,"
says Mama.

They all laugh at Mama's joke!

It was the first day of spring in Bear Country. The last patches of winter snow were melting in the warm sun. The first spring flowers were poking up their brightly colored heads. Robins sang in the green budding trees. And at the Bear family's tree house home, the kitchen window was wide open. Papa Bear sniffed the fresh spring air as he read his newspaper at the breakfast table.

"Look at this!" he said, holding up the front page. "Mayor Honeypot says that Bear Country will have an old-fashioned Easter parade this year. There will be prizes for the best-dressed family. All are invited to attend in their brightest spring finery."

"That sounds like fun," said Mama. "It would be nice to have a reason to dress up in something special for a change."

"You said it!" said Sister. "I can wear a big Easter bonnet with all kinds of fancy frills, bows, and feathers."

But Brother Bear wasn't so sure. He was happy wearing his plain red shirt and blue pants every day.

"What's the matter with our regular clothes?" he said. "Why do we have to get dressed up?"

"Oh, don't be a stick in the mud!" said Sister. "It's fun to do something different once in a while."

"I don't think so," he said. "I like things to be the same."

"But we wear the same kind of clothes every day," said Sister. "Don't you get tired of that?"

"Nope," said Brother. "That way, I always look like me."

Sister sighed and rolled her eyes.

"I would like to get out my fancy old duds," said Papa. "Remember the clothes I wore when we got married, my dear?"

"I do, indeed," said Mama. "You looked very handsome."

"I'll bet they're still up in the attic," said Papa. "Let's go take a look."

Papa led the way. Even Brother wanted to see what Papa looked like in his "fancy old duds."

The attic was full of all kinds of things the Bear family was saving. Papa opened a big dusty trunk.

"Here it is!" said Papa, pulling out his old suit jacket and putting it on.

It was a little moth-eaten and much too tight. When Papa tried to close it, a button popped off and shot across the room.

"Whoa, there, buddy!" said Mama. "You're going to put someone's eye out."

Sister poked around in the trunk and found a fancy hat. She put it on and looked at herself in a cracked mirror.

"That belonged to Grizzly Gran when she was young," said Mama.

"It's beautiful," said Sister. "But it is sort of falling apart."

Bits of ribbon and feathers were coming off.

"These fancy clothes are very nice," said Mama. "But I don't think we can wear them in the Easter parade. They're just too old. We'll have to go out and buy brand-new outfits."

"Oh, no!" Brother groaned. "Clothes shopping—boring!"

"Speak for yourself," said Sister, heading downstairs.

So in spite of Brother's moans and groans, they all got into the family car and headed to the Bear Country Mall to buy new things for the Easter parade.

The mall was full of bears busily shopping for spring clothes. Mama led them into a big department store.

"May I help you, madam?" asked a clerk.

"You certainly may," said Mama. "My whole family needs new clothes for the Easter parade."

The clerk called for help, and soon Mama, Papa, Sister, and even Brother were trying on new clothes.

They all looked splendid in their new Easter outfits. But Brother didn't think so.

"I look silly," he muttered, looking in the mirror.

"I think you look very handsome," said Sister.

"Ugh!" said Brother.

As they drove home with their car full of boxes and bags, Brother was still grumpy and frowning.

"Come, now, Brother," said Papa. "I'm sure you'll feel different on Easter Sunday when everyone in Bear Country will be dressed in their finest for the big parade."

"Hmmph!" Brother said.

Papa sighed and rolled his eyes.

Easter Sunday soon arrived,
and after church . . .

. . . and a little Easter candy,

the Bear family got ready for the parade. Brother was very unhappy about having to wear a tie.

"I can't tie this thing," he growled.

"I'll show you how," said Papa. "Around and around, and up and through."

Soon they were ready.

"My!" said Mama, looking them over proudly. "What a beautiful family I have."

"My tie is too tight!" complained Brother.

Mama sighed and rolled her eyes.

When they drove into Bear Town for the start of the parade, it was quite a sight. Hundreds of bears all in their Easter best lined Main Street. Mayor and Mrs. Honeypot were up on a reviewing stand to pick out the best outfits.

A brass band came marching by. Officer Marguerite directed traffic. Chief Bruno was dressed as the Easter Bunny and handed out candy.

The mayor gave the signal for the starting-line ribbon to be cut. Everyone streamed past the reviewing stand. The band played an old tune called "Easter Parade."

When the Bear family marched proudly past, Brother overheard Mrs. Honeypot. "Don't they all look darling!" she said. "Especially that cute little Brother Bear."

Brother blushed right through his fur.

But then he caught sight of himself in a store window.
"I guess I do look pretty good!" he said to himself.

After they had all filed past, the mayor called the Bear family up to the reviewing stand. He held out a big shiny trophy.

"And the prize for best-dressed family," said the mayor, "goes to . . . the Bear family!"

The whole crowd cheered and clapped. Brother stepped right up to take the prize. He was very pleased with himself.

"Thank you! Thank you, everyone!" he said, taking a bow.

The rest of the family just sighed and rolled their eyes.

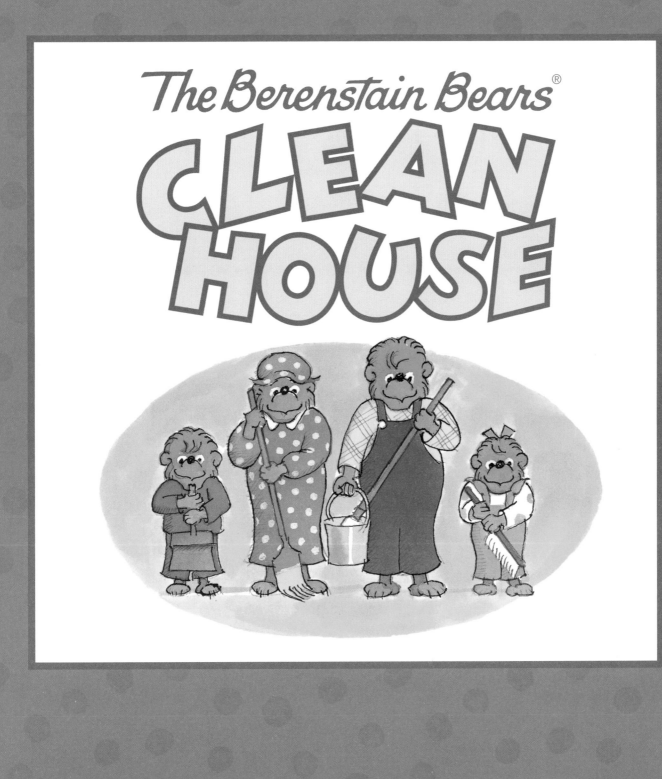

"It is spring," said Mama Bear.

"It is time to clean our house."

"I will help," said Papa.

"I will help," said Brother.

"I will help," said Sister.

"Good," said Mama.

"We will clean our house

from the top to the bottom,

from the bottom to the top."

They started at the bottom.

"My goodness," said Mama.

"There are too many things.

It is hard to clean with so many things."

"We will have a yard sale," said Papa.

"We will put some in the yard."

"This old fish," said Brother.

"It is dusty."

"This stuffed owl," said Sister.

"It is musty."

"This old fishing pole,"
said Mama.
"It is bent."

"Those are my things,"
said Papa.
"But it is spring.
We must clean house.
I will put them in
the yard."

67

They went upstairs to the living room.

"There are too many things," said Papa.

"We must put some in the yard,"
said Mama.

"This old lamp," said Brother.

"It has a crack."

"This old pillow," said Sister.

"It has a spot on the back."

"This old stool," said Papa.

"It has a tear."

"Those are my things,"
said Mama.
"But I will put them
in the yard."

Then they went upstairs.

Brother and Sister's room had many,
many things.

"My goodness!" said Mama.

"There are too many things in this room.

We must put some in the yard."

"This baseball bat," said Papa.

"It is split."

"This teddy bear," said Mama.

"The stuffing is coming out of it."

"These old games
and toys," said Papa.
"They would be fun
for other girls and boys."

"Those are our things,"
said Brother and Sister.
"We will put them
in the yard."

"Yes, it is spring," said Mama.

"We must clean our house

from the top to the bottom,

from the bottom to the top."

But there was something they forgot!

They forgot the attic!

"My goodness!" said Mama.

"We forgot the attic."

They went up to the attic.

It was bad.

"My goodness!" said Mama.

"There are too many things!"

"Yes," said Papa.

"Many, too many

to put in the yard."

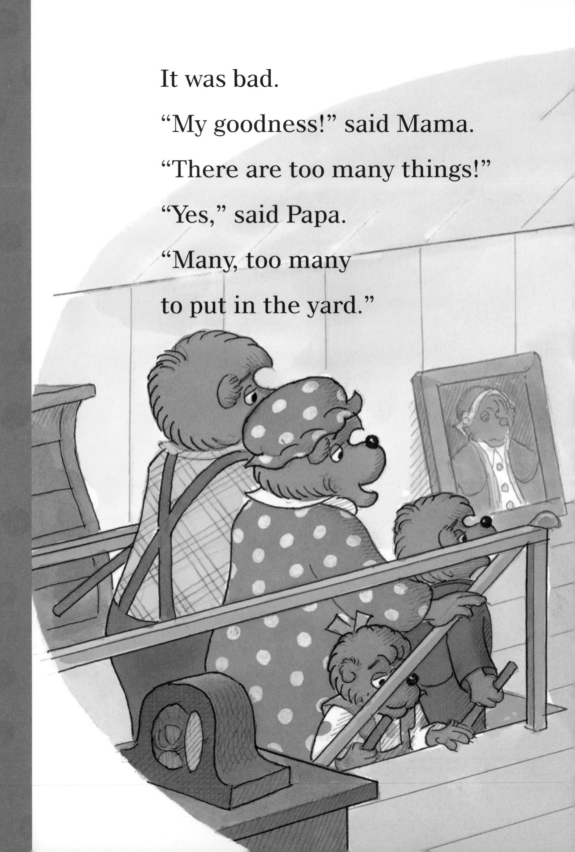

They went downstairs.

They went out to
the yard.

They made a sign.

It said YARD SALE TODAY.

They looked at the things
they put in the yard.

"This is hard," said Papa.
"I love those things
I put in the yard."

"This is hard," said Mama.

"I love those things
I put in the yard."

"This is hard,"
said Brother and Sister.

"We love those things
we put in the yard."

They took them up
to the attic.

84

They put them with the other
old things they loved.

"We have done our job," said Mama.

"But we are not done," said Brother.
"We have not cleaned the attic," said
Sister.

"We are done," said Mama.

"But the attic will not go away.

We will clean the attic

another day."

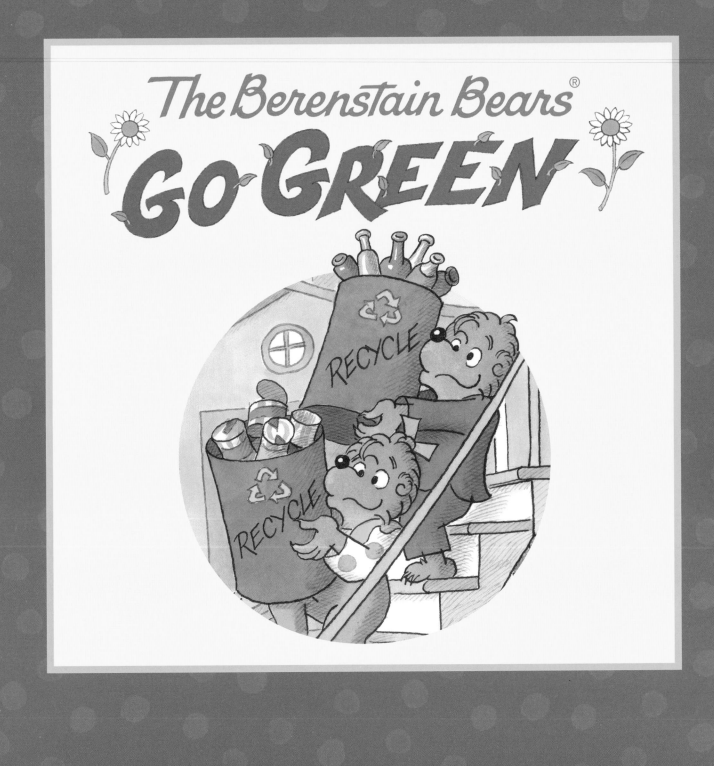

Bear Country was a beautiful place to live. It had green rolling hills and wide river valleys. It had cool shady woods and bright sunny fields.

There were steep cliffs and deep canyons, roaring rapids and rushing waterfalls.

Lots of creatures lived in Bear Country besides bears. There were deer and ducks, woodchucks and weasels. There were rabbits and raccoons, possums and porcupines.

There were badgers, bats, butterflies, bugs, and much, much more.

The Bear family loved living in Bear Country. They always tried their best to keep it beautiful. Most of the other creatures who lived there tried their best, too. But no matter how hard you try, sometimes you run into problems. And that's just what happened.

One fine morning the Bear family decided to go fishing.

"Let's go down to the creek where Grizzly Gramps keeps his boat," said Papa. "We can pack a lunch and have a picnic as we fish."

"Terrific!" they all agreed.

The family packed up their fishing gear and their lunch and went down to the creek, where they loaded into Grizzly Gramps's boat. Papa got out the oars and rowed everyone lazily along, their fishing lines out, while they ate a picnic lunch. The sun was shining, the birds were singing, and all seemed right in Bear Country.

Until . . .

GRAMPS' BOAT

"Pew!" said Sister. "What's that awful smell?"
The rest of the family sat up and sniffed.
"Yuck!" they all cried. "What is that?"

They noticed something funny floating in the water. It was a streak of dark, gunky-looking stuff. It seemed to be coming from around a bend in the creek.

"Uh-oh!" said Papa. "I know what's around that bend!"

Soon they could all see it: the Bear Country Dump!

"Wow!" said Brother. "What a mess!"

It was indeed a mess. There were wrecked cars, old mattresses, busted TV sets, broken washing machines, and piles of trash and garbage. But the worst mess was the bunch of leaky old oil drums that someone had dumped right on the edge of the creek. Gooey, smelly, black oil was leaking into the water.

"This is a disgrace!" said Mama. She hated to see her beloved Bear Country treated this way. Mama had even been the mayor of Bear Country for a time. "This has got to be cleaned up!" she said. "We will go to the town meeting and complain."

"Yes!" said Brother.

"Go, Mama!" said Sister.

"Go! Go!" said Honey.

At the next town meeting, the Bear family and many other bears filled the town hall. Mayor Honeypot was on the stage. He rapped on the desk with a gavel.

"Ahem!" he said. "The meeting is called to order. Is there any new business?"

Mama stood up to speak. But another bear jumped up before her.

"Mr. Mayor," he said, "I am Mr. Greenwood, and I have come to complain about the disgraceful state of the Bear Country Dump!"

Mama sat down to listen.

"Oil is leaking from the dump into the creek," said Mr. Greenwood. "What are you going to do about it, Mr. Mayor?"

Mayor Honeypot was surprised.

"I did not know about that," he said. "We will have a cleanup of the dump right away. Will any of you here volunteer to help?"

Everyone at the meeting raised their hands. Especially Mama, Papa, and the cubs!

A few days later, it seemed like most of Bear Country was down at the dump. Everyone pitched in to clean up the trash and junk. Much of it would be mixed with earth so that trees could grow on it. They hauled away the oil drums and put them in a safer spot far from the creek.

As the Bear family headed for home, Sister was thoughtful.

"You know," she said, "it's good to clean up the dump, but there's lots more we can do to make Bear Country clean and green. We can do things right at home. We've been learning about it in school."

"Like what?" asked Papa.

"Well," began Sister, "we can recycle and compost."

"We can stop wasting water and energy at home," added Brother.

"And," put in Mama, "we can carpool with other families going to school or shopping so we won't waste gas."

But Papa had the best "going green" idea of all. He rigged up a windmill on top of his workshop to power some of his tools.

"I think wind power is the best kind of energy there is," he explained. "It's clean, it's there any windy day you want it, and best of all," he added, "it's absolutely, totally *free*!"

"Wheee!" said Honey, holding up a pinwheel to catch the wind.

Papa Bear loved to fish.

He fished with a fancy rod
and reel.

He caught lots of big fish.

Brother, Sister, and Honey

loved to fish, too.

They fished with plain poles and lines.

They caught lots of little fish.

One day, the cubs went fishing.

Papa saw them going.

"I will go with you," he said.

"I will show you how to catch

big fish!"

They went down to the pond.

Papa fished with his fancy

rod and reel.

Brother, Sister, and Honey fished

with their plain poles and lines.

"I have a bite!" called Papa.

His rod bent over.

"It must be a big one!" he said.

He pulled in his line.

It was hard to do.

But it turned out to be just

an old boot.

"We have bites, too!" called

Brother, Sister, and Honey.

They pulled in their lines.

They caught three nice little fish.

"Hmm!" said Papa.

He fished some more.

He got another bite.

His rod bent over again.

He pulled in his line.

He pulled really hard.

But all he caught
was an old tire.

Brother, Sister, and Honey
caught more fish.
They caught lots of
nice little fish.

"Grrr!" said Papa.

He grabbed his rod.

He threw out his line . . . *far!*

"I have another bite!"

called Papa. "It is a big one!"

He tried to pull in his line.

But he could not pull it in.

Papa got yanked into the water.

He made a big splash!

"Look!" said the cubs.
"Your splash scared a
big fish out of the water."

Papa and the cubs took
the big fish home to Mama.
"Look what Papa caught!"
said the cubs.

The cubs were proud of their fisherman papa!

The Berenstain Bears®
We Love Our Mom!

It was springtime in Bear Country and everything was fresh and fragrant. The trees were budding in bright springtime green. The lilacs were in full bloom. Early butterflies flitted from tulip to daffodil, and all the mothers of Bear Country were busy taking care of their little ones.

Mama Robin was feeding worms to her chirping little fledglings. Mama Rabbit was teaching her baby bunnies how to hop. Mama Frog was taking a jar full of tadpoles out for a stroll. And in the Bear family's tree house, Mama Bear was taking care of her cubs.

It was breakfast time, and Mama was cooking
pancakes for the family. Mama's pancakes not only
tasted good, they looked good, too. She made them
into little bear faces for Brother, Sister, and Honey.
They always liked to eat the ears off first.

"Thank you, Mama," they sang,
pouring lots of honey on their
steaming-hot pancakes.

Mama Bear took care of her cubs in plenty of other ways, too. She washed their clothes. She sewed their buttons back on their clothes when they popped off. She bandaged their boo-boos when they skinned their knees or stubbed their toes.

She gave them baths, read them stories, and tucked them in at night. She gave them hugs when they woke up with bad dreams. All day, every day, Mama Bear was there for her cubs.

"Well, I'm off to Grizzly Gran's," said Papa, finishing up his breakfast. "A rocker on her favorite rocking chair came loose and I fixed it for her."

"Can we come?" asked Sister and Brother.

"Of course," said Papa. "Grizzly Gran and Gramps will be very glad to see you."

Papa loaded the rocking chair, and they all set off.

"Look at all the springtime babies and their moms," said Sister.

"Spring is a time for new babies," said Papa, "and for their mothers, too. And don't forget, Mother's Day is coming up."

Brother and Sister had forgotten about Mother's Day. They needed to figure out what they were doing for their mama on her special day.

"Howdy, grandcubs!" said Grizzly Gramps when they arrived. "Always great to see you!"

Gran tried out her rocking chair. "Why, it's as good as new," she said. "Thank you, son—you're so good to me!"

"Gee, Ma," said Papa. "It was just a loose rocker."

"Well, little things like that mean a lot to us moms."
Gran smiled and gave Papa a kiss. "Now cubs, come
look at what I'm working on." She had a big scrapbook
out on the table.

"This is my Mama's Book," she explained. "It holds so many good memories." She pointed to a picture of a pretty young bear holding a baby. "Like this . . ."

"Who's that?" asked Brother.

"That's me." Gran smiled.

"You look so young!" said Sister.

"I *was* young!" Gran laughed. "That's your father when he was born."

"Our father?" they said. "You mean *Papa*?"

"Of course," said Gran.

"But he's so little!" they both said.

"Yes," agreed Gran. "He *has* grown."

"Well, Ma," said Papa, "we've got to go. But we'll see
you next week on Mother's Day. We're all going out to
brunch at the Old Grizzly Inn."

On the way home, Brother and Sister thought about
their day. That scrapbook and Papa doing nice things
meant so much to Gran.

"We need to do something special for Mama on
Mother's Day," said Sister.

"How about making a Mama's Book like Gran's?"
suggested Papa. "You could put together a scrapbook all
about being a mother."

"Yes!" said Brother. "We can use family photos from the old box in the closet."

"A Mama's Book for our own Mama Bear," said Sister, nodding.

When they got home, Brother and Sister sneaked the box of photos out of the closet, took it to their room, and got to work. They spread the pictures on the floor and went through them. They used one of their school notebooks for a scrapbook.

They picked and chose, cut and pasted, lettered and colored, and by suppertime they were done. They hid the finished scrapbook away in a drawer. They couldn't wait for Mother's Day to arrive!

A week later, Brother, Sister, Papa, and Honey ran into Mama and Papa's room first thing in the morning.

"Happy Mother's Day!" they called. "Here's your present, Mama."

"For me?" said Mama sleepily. "How nice!" And she unwrapped her present.

"Why, it's a Mama's Book just like Gran's," she said. "How wonderful! I've always wanted one like it. Thank you, my dears!" And she gave all of them a big hug and a kiss. Then she opened the book to the first page.

Mama's Book

It had pictures of Mama with her three babies: Brother, Sister, and Honey.

"You were so cute, Brother," said Mama. "So round and plump. We called you Chubby Cubby."

Sister laughed.

"But, you, Sister," said Mama, "you cried all the time. We called you Cranky Paws."

It was Brother's turn to laugh.

"Then Honey came along," said Mama. "She was so sweet we just called her Honey."

Mama and Brother (2 weeks)

Honey pointed to her picture. "Baby!" she said.

Mama and Sister (1 week)

Mama and Honey (2 days)

The rest of the scrapbook was full of all kinds of pictures of the family. There was Brother learning to ride a bike, Sister on her first day of school, and Honey waving.

There were birthdays, picnics, vacations, school plays, soccer games, and Thanksgiving dinners. They were all the things that Mama would want to remember about her cubs growing up.

There was a tear in Mama's eye when she came to the end.

"Thank you, my dears!" she said again, hugging them all.
"This is the most wonderful Mother's Day gift I have ever gotten!"

"Happy Mother's Day, Mama!" Brother and Sister said.

"Happy!" said Honey.

"And now," said Papa, "it's time for us all to get ready to take
Mama and Gran out for their Mother's Day brunch."

And that is exactly what they did.

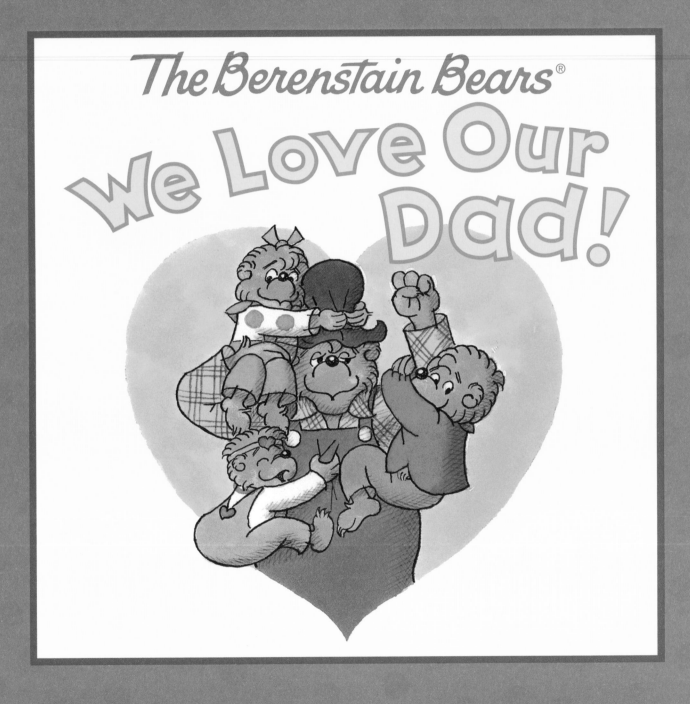

Sister, Brother, and Honey Bear loved their Papa. They loved him very much. After all, he was always there for them.

He baited their hooks when they went fishing. He threw them fly balls when they played catch. He was their sled-puller on their way to the top of Dead Bear Hill.

He carried them on his shoulders when they got tired and rushed them to the doctor when they were hurt.

He told them funny stories and corny jokes. He read to them at bedtime, tucked them in, and kissed them good night.

Yes, the cubs certainly loved their Papa Bear. But sometimes they took him a bit for granted. After all, he was always there. They never even noticed some of the things he did—like working. Papa worked very hard. He worked in his shop all day making furniture. He worked fixing things up around the house.

He worked doing chores like mowing the lawn or shoveling snow or taking out the trash. It's true that Papa enjoyed working. But he enjoyed getting credit for it sometimes, too.

One warm spring morning, not long after Mother's Day, the cubs were talking about what they would do for Father's Day. Mama was listening to them nearby.

"Let's make Papa a big family album with pictures of us doing stuff with him," said Sister.

"We just gave Mama an album like that for Mother's Day," said Brother.

"Oh, yeah," said Sister. Honey Bear was looking out the window watching Papa mowing the lawn.

"Papa workin'," she said.

"What's that, Honey?" asked Mama.

"Papa workin'!" said Honey, pointing.

"Hmm!" said Mama. "Honey just had a good idea."

"She did?" said Brother and Sister.

"Yes," said Mama. "Your Papa works very hard. It would be a nice gift if you cubs did his jobs for him on Father's Day and let him relax."

Now that they thought about it, it was true—Papa did work all the time. He could use a rest.

"Way to go, Honey Bear!" said Sister and Brother, giving her high fives.

The cubs decided to make gift certificates that Papa could cash in for the jobs they would do.

All that day, they followed him around, spying on him. They checked off the jobs he did on a clipboard.

"Carrying wood," said Sister.

"Carrying wood. Check!" said Brother.

"Check!" said Honey.

"Painting the garage," said Sister.

"Painting the garage. Check!" said Brother.

"Check!" said Honey.

"Replacing loose tree bark on tree house," said
Sister.
"Replacing loose tree bark. Check!" said Brother.
"Check!" said Honey.

The cubs followed Papa the next day, too. They didn't put furniture making on their list because they didn't know how to make furniture.

But they did check off things like trimming the rose bushes, putting up fence rails, and cleaning out the basement.

That evening, they made a gift certificate for each job.
The cubs couldn't wait for Father's Day to arrive so they could
surprise him with their special gift!

On Father's Day, the cubs woke up bright and early. They waited until nearly six a.m. before running into Mama and Papa's room and jumping on the bed.

"Happy Father's Day, Papa!" they yelled.

"Huh? Wha?" said Papa, sleepily. "Is it Father's Day?"

"Of course it is!" said the cubs. "Open your present!" They gave him a big envelope. Papa thought it was a card.

"Why, thank you," he said. But when he opened it, the gift certificates spilled out.

"What's this?" he asked.

"They're gift certificates you cash in for us to do your jobs," explained Brother. "You can just relax all day."

"What a thoughtful gift," said Papa.

"It was Honey's idea," said Sister.

"Thank you, Honey!" said Papa, giving all his thoughtful cubs a big hug.

"I think I'd like to spend the day just watching baseball," said Papa. "It's Father's Day," said Mama. "You can do whatever you like." "Wow!" said Papa, settling down in his easy chair in front of the TV. "I could get used to this."

Papa cashed in his gift certificates and the cubs set to work. Their first job was washing the car. They got out buckets, soap, cloths, and the garden hose. They scrubbed and washed and rinsed. But the car still seemed a little dirty.

"Papa!" they called. "We're having trouble. Can you help us?"

"Of course," he said, looking things over. "You just need more elbow grease. I'll show you."

So Papa and the cubs scrubbed and washed and rinsed together. When they were done, the car was bright and clean and shiny.

"You go and relax now, Papa," said the cubs. "We'll do the rest."

Their next job was cleaning up the wood chips in Papa's shop. The cubs got out dust pans, brooms, and a shop vacuum and set to work. They swept and cleaned and vacuumed. But the shop still looked a little dirty.

"Papa!" they called. "We're having trouble. Can you help us?"

"Of course," he said, looking things over. "You just need to give it more oomph! I'll show you."

So Papa and the cubs swept and cleaned and vacuumed together. When they were done, the shop was spic and span.

"You go and relax now, Papa," said the cubs. "We'll do the rest."

Their next job was spreading grass seed on the bare spots in the lawn. The cubs got out rakes and bags of seed. Brother raked the hard-packed earth while Sister and Honey spread the seed. But they soon got tired. There were still a lot of bare spots left.

"Papa!" they called. "We're having trouble. Can you help us?"

"Of course," he said, looking things over. "You just need more muscle power. I'll show you."

So Papa and the cubs raked and spread the seed. When they were done, every bare spot on the lawn was covered with new seed.

"You go and relax now, Papa," said the cubs. "We'll do the rest." But Papa shook his head.

"Actually," he said, "I'm getting bored just watching TV. It's more fun doing things with you. What shall we do next?"

"How about a game of baseball?" said Brother.

"Perfect!" said Papa.

So the whole family played ball. Brother, Sister, and Honey took turns pitching, batting, and fielding. Papa was catcher and Mama was the ump. A wonderful Father's Day was had by all!

At bedtime, the cubs took turns jumping
off their beds onto a big cushion.

"It isn't fair!" said Brother as Papa helped him into his pajamas. "There's a Mother's Day and a Father's Day—why isn't there a Cubs' Day?"

Papa smiled at Mama Bear.

"I haven't the faintest idea," he said.

Papa and Mama tucked the cubs in and turned out the light.

"Did you have a good Father's Day, Papa?" asked Sister.

"Yes, sweetie," said Papa, kissing her, Brother, and Honey good night. "The best Father's Day ever!"